PAULINA
is thoughtful
and responsible.
Sometimes she's
like a second mom
to her friends.
Violet
is gentle and shy.
Because of this, she
can be taken to be
a bit of a snobby
rodent.
Turtle Island's
beaches and caves
make wonderful
nesting grounds for
its population of sea
turtles!

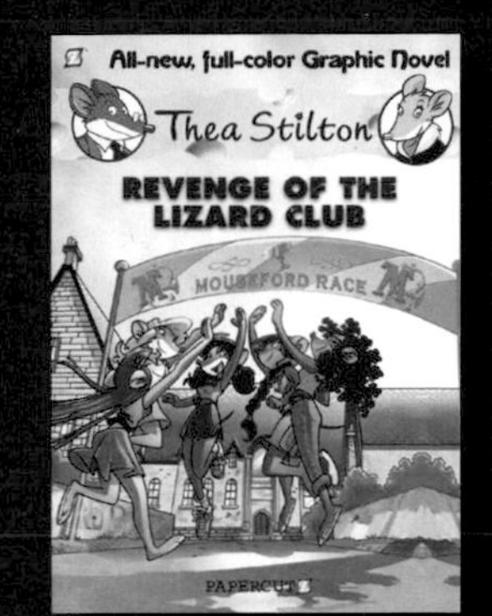

Graphic Novel #2
"Revenge of the Lizard Club"

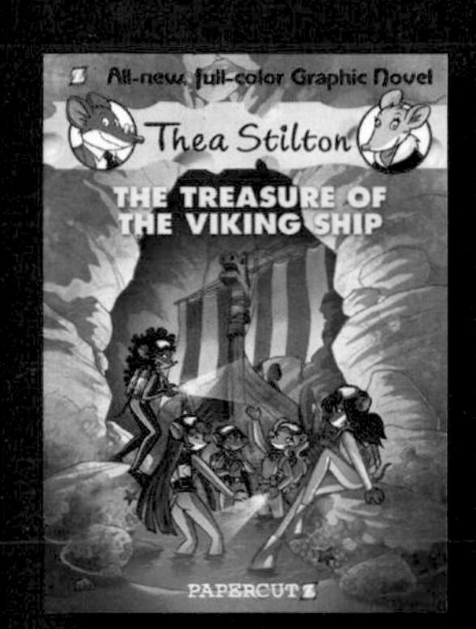

Graphic Novel #3
"The Treasure of the Viking Ship"

Graphic Novel #4
"Catching the

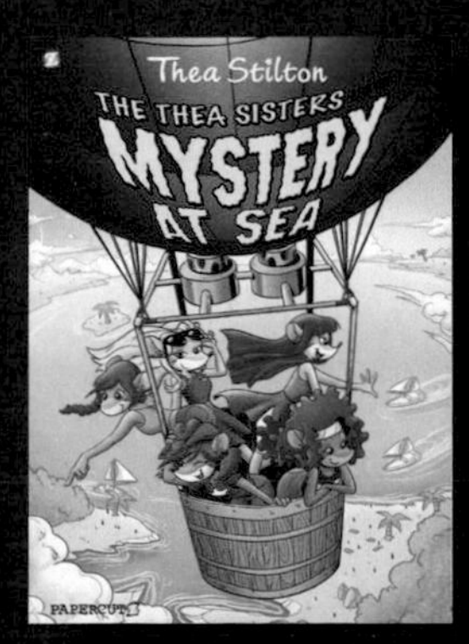

COMING SOON

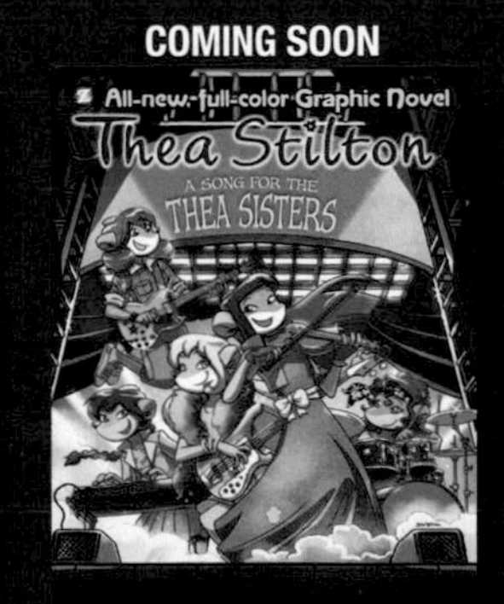

PAPERCUTZ

Thea Stilton

PAPERCUTZ™

Thea Stilton

THE THEA SISTERS AND THE MYSTERY AT SEA!

By Thea Stilton

New York

THEA STILTON #6
THE THEA SISTERS AND THE MYSTERY AT SEA!

Text by Thea Stilton
Cover by Ryan Jampole (artist) and Matt Herms (colorist)
Project Supervision by Alessandra Berello (Atlantyca S.p.A.)
Script by Franceso Savino
Translation by Nanette McGuinness
Art by Ryan Jampole
Color by Dave Tanguay, Laurie Smith, and Matteo Baldrighi
Letters by Wilson Ramos

Dawn Guzzo- Production
Brittanie Black – Production Coordinator
Rachel Gluckstern – Editor
Jeff Whitman – Assistant Managing Editor
Jim Salicrup
Editor-in-Chief

ISBN: 978-1-62991-478-7

Printed in China.
August 2016 by WKT Co. LTD.
3/F Phase 1 Leader Industrial Centre
188 Texaco Road, Tsuen Wan, N.T.
Hong Kong

Distributed by Macmillan
First Printing

SO THE PLAN IS CLEAR? ARE YOU READY TO SPRING INTO ACTION?
IT LOOKS LIKE COSMETICS QUEEN VISSIA DE VISSEN IS ABOUT TO COMMIT MORE MISCHIEF. WILL THE THEA SISTERS BE ABLE TO STOP HER THIS TIME?
HEY, WAIT A MINUTE . . . WHAT'S GOING ON?
PAULINA, PAM, AND *COLETTE* ARE HELPING *VISSIA DE VISSEN?*
YES, MS. DE VISSEN! YOU CAN COUNT ON US!
DON'T FORGET! THIS MISSION IS OF THE UTMOST IMPORTANCE!
TO FIND OUT, WE'LL HAVE TO GO BACK A FEW DAYS . . .

. . . TO THE DAY OF THE HOT-AIR BALLOON RIDE ARRANGED BY MOUSEFORD ACADEMY!
EVERY YEAR, THE BIOLOGY TEACHER, PROFESSOR VAN KRAKEN, FLIES HIS STUDENTS OVER THE WHALE ISLAND ARCHIPELAGO!
LOOK!, PAMELA FROM UP HERE, WHALE ISLAND SEEMS SO TINY!
WOW, YOU'RE RIGHT, NICKY!
IT'S AMAZING TO SEE EVERYTHING FROM ABOVE. DON'T YOU AGREE, COLETTE?
YES, YES, WHAT YOU SAID--BUT DOESN'T ANYBODY CARE ABOUT ALL THIS WIND THAT'S MESSING UP MY HAIR?

SOON, WE'LL BE FLYING OVER TURTLE ISLAND, FAMOUS FOR THE LARGE NUMBER OF MARINE TURTLES WHO NEST ON ITS SHORELINE!
A-A-AND THEN WE'LL GO BACK HOME, RIGHT, PROFESSOR VAN KRANKEN?
WHAT'S UP, SHEN? YOU'RE NOT AFRAID, ARE YOU?
WHO, ME?! I WAS JUST ASKING FOR OUR DE VISSON FRIENDS WHO DIDN'T WANT TO COME FLY WITH US. THEY MIGHT BE GETTING WORRIED!
VIC, I DON'T UNDERSTAND WHY WE INSIST ON USING HOT-AIR BALLOONS, WHEN MODERN TECHNOLOGY HAS GIVEN US PRIVATE HELICOPTERS!
RELAX, VANILLA! THIS ALL HAS A CERTAIN CHARM, DON'T YOU THINK?
SURE . . . IF ONLY WE DIDN'T HAVE TO FLY WITH *THEM*.
PROFESSOR, COME LOOK!
ISN'T ***THAT*** TURTLE ISLAND?
YES, VIOLET, BUT . . .

LOOK AT ALL THAT GARBAGE!
AND WHERE ARE THE TURTLES?!
PROFESSOR, I THINK WE'D BETTER GO DOWN! WE HAVE TO FIGURE OUT WHAT'S GOING ON!
VANILLA, DO YOU KNOW ANYTHING ABOUT THIS? IF THIS IS MORE OF OUR MOTHER'S MISCHIEF, THIS WON'T GO SO GOOD FOR US!
NO, I DON'T KNOW, VIC BUT WE SHOULD PLAY ALONG FOR NOW--LET'S ACT INTERESTED!
LET'S CHECK! PREPARE FOR LANDING!

SOON...
I'VE CHANGED MY MIND. I THINK I'M REALLY AFRAID NOW!
KEEP CALM, SHEN. I HAVE EVERYTHING UNDER CONTROL. IT'LL BE A TOP-NOTCH EMERGENCY LANDING!
ARE YOU SURE THIS WAS A GOOD IDEA, GIRLS? WE'RE DROPPING PRETTY FAST!
IT'LL BE A LITTLE ROCKY, BUT EVERYTHING'LL BE OKAY!
WHAT DO YOU MEAN, "IT'LL BE A LITTLE ROCKY?"
AAAH!
THUMP

IS EVERYONE OKAY?
WE ARE . . .
. . . BUT THE ISLAND ISN'T.
VANILLA, COME LOOK! THERE'S CLEARLY SOMEONE RESPONSIBLE FOR THIS TRASH!
R.M.--RICHARD MALEFACTOR! TO BLAME!
RICHARD MALEFACTOR? WHO'S THAT?
RM
I KNOW SOMEONE WHO'LL WANT TO COME HERE IN PERSON AND TELL EVERYONE ABOUT IT!
LET'S KEEP OUR EYES OPEN, GIRLS! I WANT US TO GET TO THE BOTTOM OF THIS!
WHAT'S GOING ON, PAULINA?
I DON'T KNOW, NICKY, BUT THIS TIME IT SEEMS LIKE VISSIA HAS NOTHING TO DO WITH IT . . .

A FEW MINUTES LATER, A VERY IMPORTANT PERSON ARRIVES AT TURTLE ISLAND . . .
. . . VISSIA DE VISSEN!
WHO COULD HAVE SPOILED THIS MARVELOUS BEACH? A UNIQUE VISTA RUINED BY THE WORST KIND OF SCOUNDREL!
NOT TO MENTION THE POOR SEA TURTLES!
YES, YES, OF COURSE, NATURALLY--THE TURTLES! I WAS THINKING ABOUT THE POOR TURTLES!
VISSIA HAS NO IDEA WHAT SHE'S TALKING ABOUT. SHE JUST CAME HERE TO GET PUBLICITY!
RIGHT. AS USUAL, THAT LADY ONLY DOES THINGS TO BENEFIT HERSELF!
SET UP THE TV CAMERAS SO I'M IN THE BEST LIGHT! MAKE SURE YOU CAN SEE THE TRASH!
AS SOON AS I SAW RICHARD MALEFACTOR'S LOGO, I KNEW YOU'D FINALLY BE ABLE TO GET YOUR REVENGE.
VERY CLEVER, VANILLA.

"THAT'S EXACTLY WHAT I INTEND TO DO, VANILLA. RICHARD'S STOLEN THE PLACE I DESERVE AS *MAKEUP MONARCH* TOO MANY TIMES!"
THIS YEAR, THE AWARD FOR THE BUSINESS-RODENT OF THE YEAR GOES TO . . . ***RICHARD MALEFACTOR!***
THANK YOU, MY ESTEEMED COLLEAGUES. IT'S A TRUE PLEASURE TO RECEIVE THIS AWARD, THE FINAL PROOF--AS IF ANY WERE NEEDED--
--OF MY UNDISPUTED SUPREMACY!
COSMETICS ARE MY WORLD, AND ***MY*** COSMETICS MAKE THE ***WORLD*** BEAUTIFUL!
"NOW THAT HIS TRASH HAS SPOILED THIS BEACH, I HAVE TO TAKE ADVANTAGE OF THE OPPORTUNITY!"

WHILE I CERTAINLY DON'T INTEND TO EXPLOIT THIS SITUATION, IT'S MY DUTY TO STEP IN AND PROTECT THIS MARVELOUS SITE.
SOME PEOPLE MAY THINK THAT RICHARD MALEFACTOR IS BEHIND THIS DISTASTEFUL INCIDENT, BUT I KNOW THAT CANNOT BE SO.
RICHARD IS A RESPECTED COLLEAGUE OF MINE, AND HE WOULD NEVER DO ANYTHING LIKE THIS!
THAT'S WHY I'VE COME HERE IN PERSON TO ANNOUNCE THAT I'M STEPPING IN TO EXPOSE THE REAL CULPRIT!
WHAT A NOBLE GESTURE!
HURRAH, MS. DE VISSEN!
AND NOT JUST ME! I'LL PUT ALL MY RESOURCES AT THE DISPOSAL OF THE WHALE ISLAND COMMUNITY TO CLEAN UP THE BEACH!
WHAT DO YOU THINK, GIRLS?
I DON'T KNOW . . . A GESTURE LIKE THIS FROM VISSIA IS COMPLETELY UNEXPECTED.

FWUSH
?
NICKY, COME WITH ME!
WHAT'S UP, VIOLET?
YOU'LL SEE . . .
SEE, THERE'S AT LEAST ONE LITTLE GUY HERE.
AND HE HAS COMPANY!

WHERE ARE THEY GOING?
COULD THERE BE A HIDING PLACE SOMEWHERE AROUND HERE?
WHOA! LOOK AT THAT!
THEY'RE GOING INTO THAT GROTTO!
THAT'S *STRANGE* BEHAVIOR FOR SEA TURTLES!
LET'S TAKE A LOOK.
Oooo!

HERE'S WHERE THEY ALL ARE GOING!
LET'S GET BACK TO THE OTHERS. WE'LL FIGURE OUT WHAT TO DO TOGETHER!

AND SO . . .
WHERE'D YOU TWO GET TO?
WE FOUND THE TURTLES! THEY'RE HIDING IN A SEA GROTTO NOT FAR FROM HERE!
I THINK WE SHOULD FOLLOW THEM. I WANT TO CHECK THAT THEY'RE SAFE!
YOU'RE RIGHT, NICKY, BUT I CAN'T LET YOU GO BY YOURSELF! I'LL GO WITH YOU.
WHAT'LL WE DO ABOUT VISSIA? IN SPITE OF HOW IT LOOKS, I STILL DON'T TRUST HER!
NOW REMEMBER, FOLKS: MY LOVE OF NATURE NEEDS TO SHOW CLEARLY IN THESE PICTURES!
RM
RM

I THINK IT'D BE BETTER IF WE SPLIT UP, GIRLS.
YEAH, NICKY, VIOLET, AND THE PROFESSOR CAN FOLLOW THE TURTLES. WE'LL FOCUS ON VISSIA!
MAYBE I CAN SPY OUT SOME SECRETS ABOUT HER BEAUTY PRODUCTS!
WE'RE SUPPOSED TO CHECK ON *HER*, COLETTE-- NOT HER MAKEUP!
DON'T FORGET, GIRLS, WE'RE COUNTING ON YOU!
TRY TO STAY OUT OF TROUBLE--IF YOU CAN!
WHERE ARE *THEY* GOING?
THE THEA SISTERS MUST BE PLOTTING SOMETHING, FOR SURE. I SHOULD--
VANILLA!

I WANT YOU TO FOLLOW THOSE THREE, VANILLA I WON'T LET ANYONE GET IN MY WAY.
BUT MOM! I THOUGHT I COULD CELEBRATE YOUR VICTORY OVER MALEFACTOR WITH YOU!
IT'S IMPORTANT WE DE VISSENS MAKE SURE WE'RE AT THE FOREFRONT OF SAVING THIS ISLAND, MY DEAR.
WHAT IF YOU NEED A HAND? YOU KNOW YOU CAN'T TRUST VIC--
IF SHE DOES, WE CAN ALWAYS HELP HER!
YOU?!
IT WOULD BE A GREAT HONOR TO HELP YOU, MS. DE VISSEN!
THE THEA SISTERS, EH? WHO WOULD HAVE EXPECTED THAT?
THEY'RE NOTHING BUT POOR DUPES! IF THEY PLAN TO MAKE ME LOOK BAD IN FRONT OF MY MOM, THEY'RE SORELY MISTAKEN!
I'LL SHOW EVERYONE WHAT VANILLA DE VISSEN CAN DO!

THAT EVENING . . .
CHANNEL 6 NEWS
COSMETICS QUEEN VISSIA DE VISSEN HAS BEGUN OPERATIONS TO CLEAN UP TURTLE ISLAND.
DE VISSEN DECLARES MALEFACTOR INNOCENT
I'M POSITIVE MY COLLEAGUE MALEFACTOR IS INNOCENT, AND THAT SOMEONE SET THIS UP TO DISCREDIT HIM.
THAT JEALOUS WOMAN WOULDN'T EXPECT ANYONE ELSE!
DE VISSEN DECLARES MALEFACTOR INNOCENT
SHE DOESN'T BELIEVE I'M INNOCENT! VISSIA JUST WANTS TO PROVE MY GUILT TO LOOK GOOD IN FRONT OF THE WHOLE COMMUNITY!
SAY WHAT, BOSS? WHY WOULD SHE DO THAT?

THINK ABOUT IT, GEORGE. THIS SCHEME WOULD BE GOOD FOR HER IMAGE AND HER BUSINESS.
I HAVE TO ADMIT, IT WAS CLEVER OF HER NOT TO ATTACK ME DIRECTLY.
YEAH, BUT . . . WE REALLY *WERE* THE ONES WHO THREW THE GARBAGE INTO THE TURTLE ISLAND GROTTOS. WE DIDN'T THINK IT'D EVER COME BACK TO THE SURFACE!
OW!
WOULD YOU SHUT UP? IF THAT INFORMATION GETS INTO THE WRONG HANDS, ***IT'LL ALL BE OVER!***
I'M SURE VISSIA WILL SEARCH FOR PROOF I'M GUILTY. MAKE SURE THIS FILE ABOUT THE GARBAGE DISPOSAL STAYS SECURE, GEORGE.
OPERATION LANDFILL
NO PROBLEM, MR. MALEFACTOR. AS ***HEAD OF SECURITY***, I ASSURE YOU THAT ***NO ONE*** WILL GET THEIR PAWS ON IT!
VERY GOOD, GEORGE . . .

". . . WITHOUT THESE DOCUMENTS, VISSIA WON'T HAVE A CHANCE OF SUCCEEDING!"
WHAT DO YOU SAY, GIRLS?
ALL WE HAVE TO DO IS GO INTO MALEFACTOR'S BUILDING AND GET THE PROOF!
GIRLS, I DON'T WANT BE PART OF A PLAN WHERE WE HAVE TO *SPY* AND *STEAL!*
IT'S TRUE. WE CAN'T JUST *STEAL* THE DOCUMENTS--
COME NOW, GIRLS! I'M SURPRISED AT YOU!
DO YOU OR *DON'T* YOU WANT TO SAVE TURTLE ISLAND? THAT'S THE ONLY WAY, MY DEAR.

WHEN IT COMES TO DOING A GOOD DEED, ALL METHODS MUST BE AVAILABLE. SAVING THE ISLAND IS A GOOD DEED, DON'T YOU THINK?
WHAT IF WE JUST TAKE A PICTURE OF THE DOCUMENTS?
OOOOH, THAT SOUNDS BETTER.
SO THE PLAN IS SIMPLE: COLETTE AND PAMELA WILL SNEAK INTO MALEFACTOR'S BUILDING AND GET A PHOTO OF THE DOCUMENTS.
PAULINA WILL STAY HERE AND GUIDE THEM FROM THIS LOCATION.
WHAT DO YOU SAY, MY BRAVE THEA SISTERS?
ARE YOU READY?

MEANWHILE . . .
YES, GIRLS, YOU WERE RIGHT--IT'S AN INCREDIBLE SIGHT! THIS GROTTO IS ANCIENT, AND YET NO ONE EVER KNEW IT WAS HERE!
AND MAYBE IT'S BETTER THAT WAY.
RIGHT. HOPEFULLY, IT'S STILL POLLUTION FREE.
THERE'S ONLY ONE WAY TO FIND OUT-- EXPLORE IT!

YEAH, LET'S JUST HOPE WE DON'T GET LOST!
IT'S A LABYRINTH!
AS LONG AS WE FOLLOW THE TURTLES, WE SHOULD'T LOSE TRACK OF OUR DIRECTION.
NICKY, ARE YOU SURE YOU WANT TO COME WITH US? I KNOW YOU DON'T LIKE TIGHT SPACES.
THANKS, VIOLET. I THINK I CAN DO IT!
HEY--WHAT'S GOING ON UP AHEAD THERE?
I CAN'T SEE CLEARLY-- BUT IT DOESN'T LOOK GOOD!

I'LL GO LOOK!
BE CAREFUL, NICKY!
SPLOOSH
JUST WHAT I WAS AFRAID OF. MORE GARBAGE!
DON'T BE SCARED, LITTLE BUDDY. YOU'RE SAFE NOW!
HEH HEH!
THAT'S ENOUGH, NOW, OR I WON'T EVER WANT TO LEAVE!
IF THERE'S GARBAGE HERE, TOO, IT MEANS THIS GROTTO MUST BE CONNECTED TO SOME *OTHER* PART OF THE ISLAND.
YES. I'M AFRAID THAT MIGHT BE TRUE.
WE NEED TO GET MOVING, GIRLS. THIS ENVIRONMENTAL DISASTER IS WORSE THAN I THOUGHT!

WHILE PROFESSOR VAN KRAKEN, NICKY, AND VIOLET TRY TO FIGURE OUT WHAT'S GOING ON IN THE GROTTO, AN IMPORTANT SPY MISSION IS ABOUT TO BEGIN . . .
SO, WHAT DO YOU SAY? ARE YOU WITH ME?
YES, MS. DE VISSEN!
READY FOR MISSION TURTLE RESCUE!
GOOD. LIKE EVERY SELF-RESPECTING SECRET AGENT, YOU'LL NEED TO DISGUISE YOURSELVES. I'VE ALREADY THOUGHT OF EVERYTHING.
WHAT?! WE'RE SUPPOSED TO DELIVER . . . PIZZAS?
HEH HEH!
IT'S JUST A COVER SO YOU CAN GET IN. ONCE YOU'RE INSIDE, YOU CAN USE THESE EARPHONES TO COMMUNICATE WITH PAULINA AND FOLLOW HER DIRECTIONS.
WHAT'S THE PLAN?
OH, IT'S VERY SIMPLE . . .

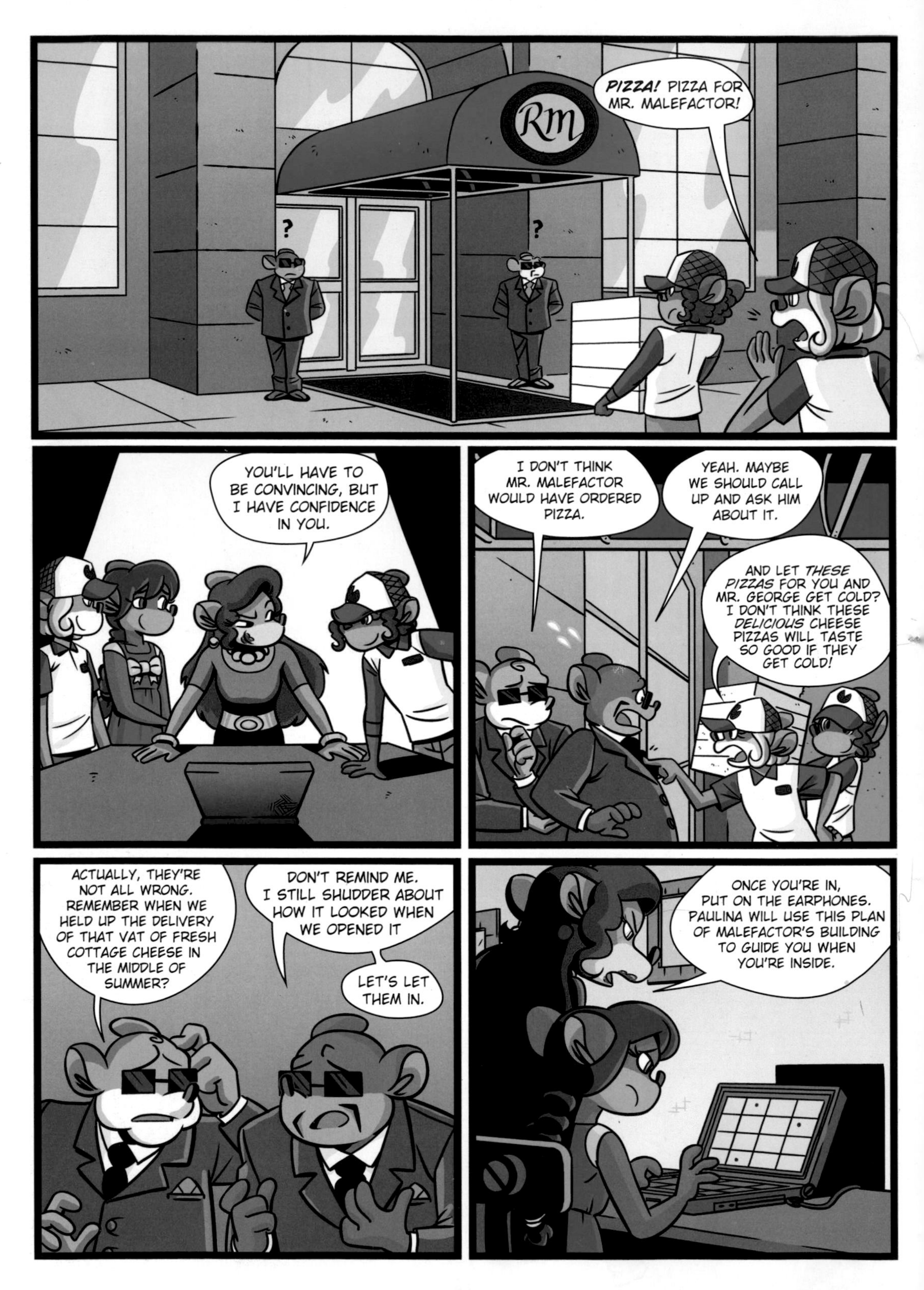
RM
PIZZA! PIZZA FOR MR. MALEFACTOR!
?
?
YOU'LL HAVE TO BE CONVINCING, BUT I HAVE CONFIDENCE IN YOU.
I DON'T THINK MR. MALEFACTOR WOULD HAVE ORDERED PIZZA.
YEAH. MAYBE WE SHOULD CALL UP AND ASK HIM ABOUT IT.
AND LET *THESE PIZZAS* FOR YOU AND MR. GEORGE GET COLD? I DON'T THINK THESE *DELICIOUS* CHEESE PIZZAS WILL TASTE SO GOOD IF THEY GET COLD!
ACTUALLY, THEY'RE NOT ALL WRONG. REMEMBER WHEN WE HELD UP THE DELIVERY OF THAT VAT OF FRESH COTTAGE CHEESE IN THE MIDDLE OF SUMMER?
DON'T REMIND ME. I STILL SHUDDER ABOUT HOW IT LOOKED WHEN WE OPENED IT
LET'S LET THEM IN.
ONCE YOU'RE IN, PUT ON THE EARPHONES. PAULINA WILL USE THIS PLAN OF MALEFACTOR'S BUILDING TO GUIDE YOU WHEN YOU'RE INSIDE.

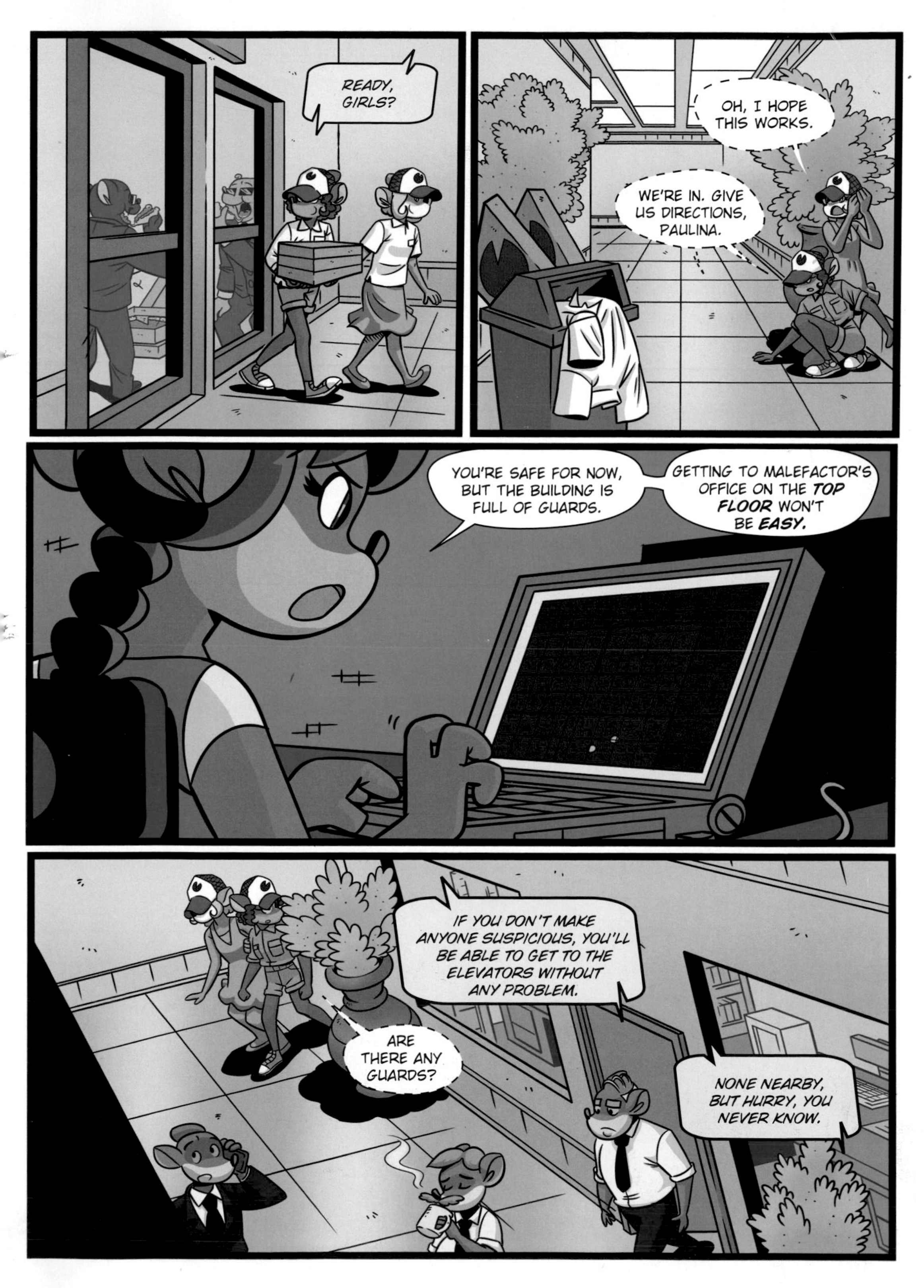
READY, GIRLS?
OH, I HOPE THIS WORKS.
WE'RE IN. GIVE US DIRECTIONS, PAULINA.
YOU'RE SAFE FOR NOW, BUT THE BUILDING IS FULL OF GUARDS.
GETTING TO MALEFACTOR'S OFFICE ON THE TOP FLOOR WON'T BE EASY.
IF YOU DON'T MAKE ANYONE SUSPICIOUS, YOU'LL BE ABLE TO GET TO THE ELEVATORS WITHOUT ANY PROBLEM.
ARE THERE ANY GUARDS?
NONE NEARBY, BUT HURRY, YOU NEVER KNOW.

TAKE THE FIRST HALLWAY ON THE RIGHT.
HUH?!
OOOH!
"THE COSMETICS CLOSET!"
MAKEUP! SO MUCH MAKEUP! I CAN'T RESIST! I JUST HAVE TO TAKE A QUICK LOOK!
COLETTE!
PAM, WHAT'S GOING ON? YOU'RE MOVING INTO AN AREA THAT'S FULL OF GUARDS!
JUST A LITTLE HITCH IN THE PLAN, PAULINA.

HOW CAN I RESIST ALL THESE GOODIES? HO-O-O-OW?
NOW'S NOT THE TIME, COLETTE! WE HAVE TO MOVE AWAY FROM HERE!
UMM . . . GIRLS? NOT TO INTERRUPT YOUR SHOPPING, BUT TWO BIG PROBLEMS ARE COMING YOUR WAY!
THIS WORK SHIFT ALWAYS WIPES ME OUT. HOW ABOUT A SNACK?
MY TREAT THIS TIME!
YUM! THEN I'LL HAVE ONE OF EACH!
GO FOR IT, BUT THE GORGONZOLA'S THE BEST!
WHEN IN DOUBT, GET THEM ALL!!
HA HA! YOU'RE UNBELIEVABLE!
WHEW! THAT WAS CLOSE!
NEXT TIME, COULD YOU TRY TO RESIST?
COULD YOU SAVE THE DISCUSSION FOR LATER, GIRLS?

YOU'RE RIGHT, PAM IT WAS MY FAULT. I WON'T DO IT AGAIN--
I HOPE NOT!
QUIET DOWN, OR THEY'LL CATCH YOU! TAKE THE EMPLOYEE ELEVATOR TO THE TOP FLOOR.
BIIING
WAIT!
BIIING
-OOF- . . . THANKS!
YOU'RE THERE, GIRLS! THE TOP FLOOR! THIS IS WHERE MALEFACTOR'S OFFICE IS!

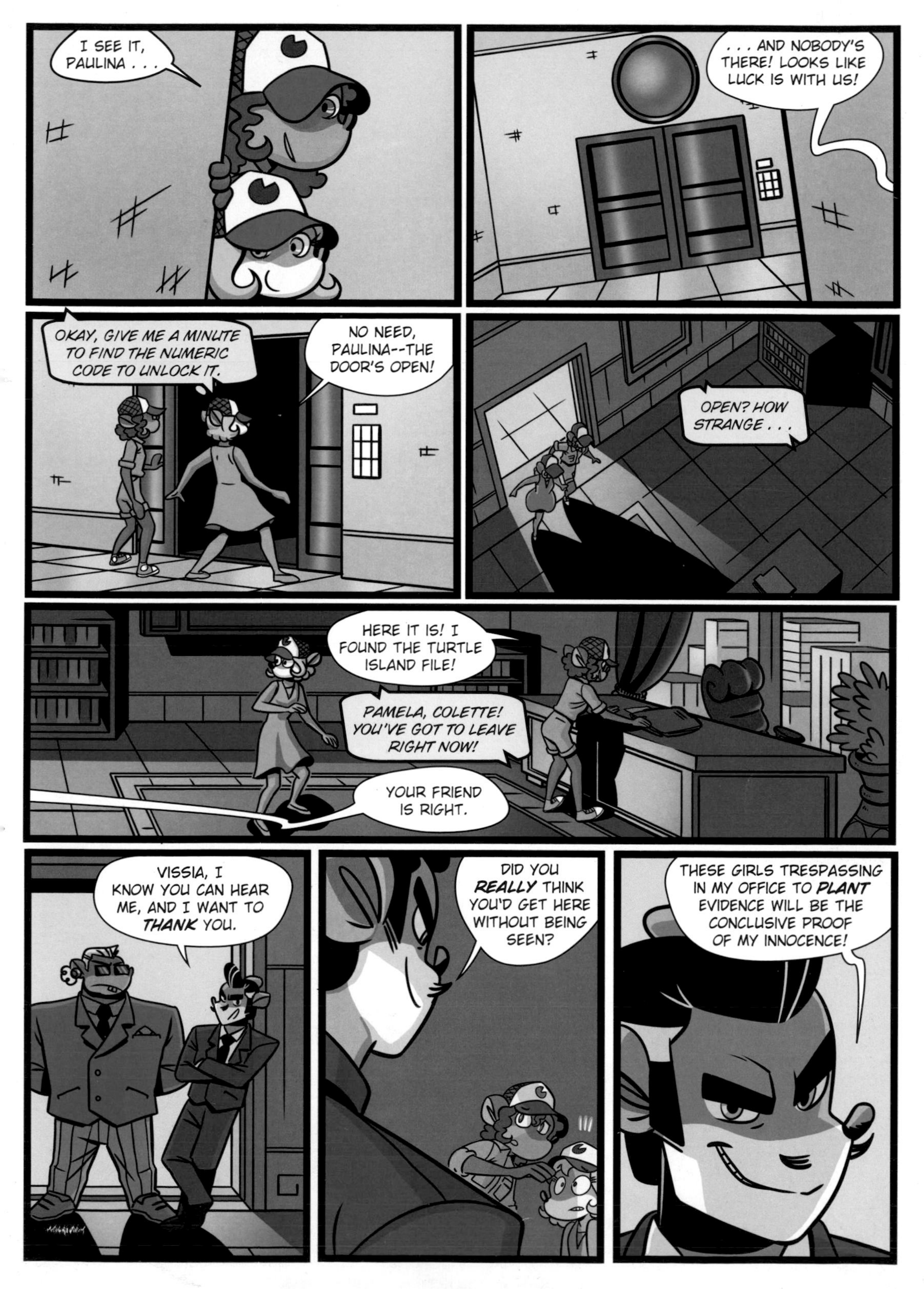
I SEE IT, PAULINA . . .
. . . AND NOBODY'S THERE! LOOKS LIKE LUCK IS WITH US!
OKAY, GIVE ME A MINUTE TO FIND THE NUMERIC CODE TO UNLOCK IT.
NO NEED, PAULINA--THE DOOR'S OPEN!
OPEN? HOW STRANGE . . .
HERE IT IS! I FOUND THE TURTLE ISLAND FILE!
PAMELA, COLETTE! YOU'VE GOT TO LEAVE RIGHT NOW!
YOUR FRIEND IS RIGHT.
VISSIA, I KNOW YOU CAN HEAR ME, AND I WANT TO THANK YOU.
DID YOU REALLY THINK YOU'D GET HERE WITHOUT BEING SEEN?
THESE GIRLS TRESPASSING IN MY OFFICE TO PLANT EVIDENCE WILL BE THE CONCLUSIVE PROOF OF MY INNOCENCE!

MEANWHILE . . .
WHAT WAS THAT? DID YOU HEAR SOMETHING?
WHOOSH WHOOSH
YES. SOMEONE'S FOLLOWING US!
LET'S HIDE BEHIND THIS ROCK!
WHAT DO WE DO?
WAIT UNTIL THEY GET PAST THE ROCK. WE'LL TAKE THEM BY SURPRISE!
3 . . .
2 . . .
AAAAH!
AAAAH!

THANK GOODNESS I FOUND YOU! I'M SO GLAD TO SEE YOU!
VANILLA? WHAT ARE YOU DOING HERE?
YOU SCARED US!
THIS GROTTO IS A MAZE FULL OF DANGERS AND MONSTERS!
THEY'RE NOT MONSTERS, THEY'RE ANIMALS! AND IF YOU HADN'T BEEEN SNEAKING AROUND AFTER US, YOU WOULDN'T HAVE GOTTEN LOST IN HERE!
I WASN'T LOST, FOR YOUR INFORMATION! I WANT TO HELP YOU WITH THE TURTLES!
SUUURE. YOU PROBABLY WANT TO CAPTURE ONE, OR . . . OR . . . WHO KNOWS WHAT?!
ALL RIGHT, ENOUGH!
HOLD ON-- WE'VE GOT A PROBLEM . . .
. . . WE CAN'T GO ANY FARTHER!
NO, REALLY?

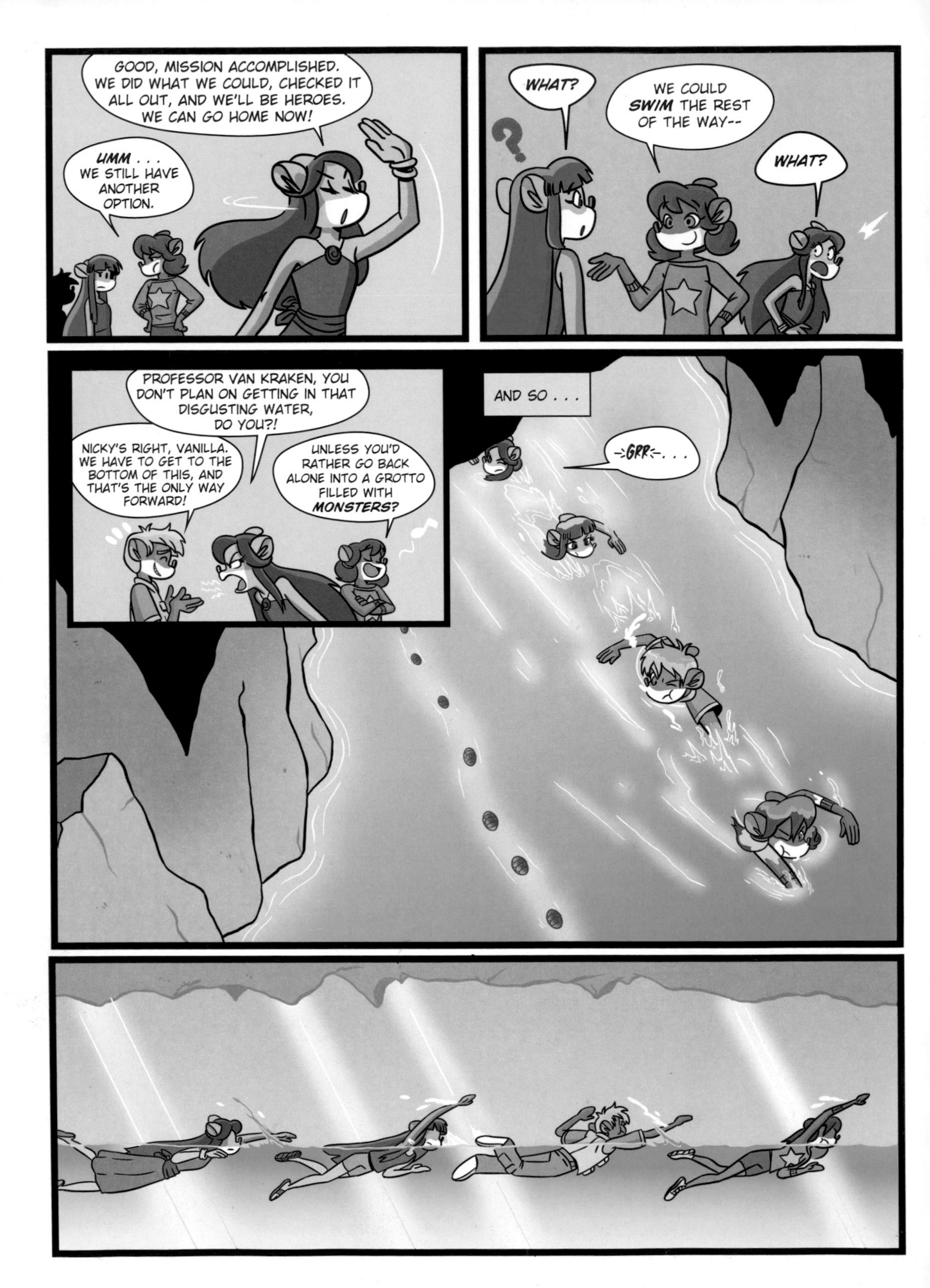
GOOD, MISSION ACCOMPLISHED. WE DID WHAT WE COULD, CHECKED IT ALL OUT, AND WE'LL BE HEROES. WE CAN GO HOME NOW!
UMM . . . WE STILL HAVE ANOTHER OPTION.
WHAT?
WE COULD SWIM THE REST OF THE WAY--
WHAT?
PROFESSOR VAN KRAKEN, YOU DON'T PLAN ON GETTING IN THAT DISGUSTING WATER, DO YOU?!
NICKY'S RIGHT, VANILLA. WE HAVE TO GET TO THE BOTTOM OF THIS, AND THAT'S THE ONLY WAY FORWARD!
UNLESS YOU'D RATHER GO BACK ALONE INTO A GROTTO FILLED WITH MONSTERS?
AND SO . . .
GRR . . .

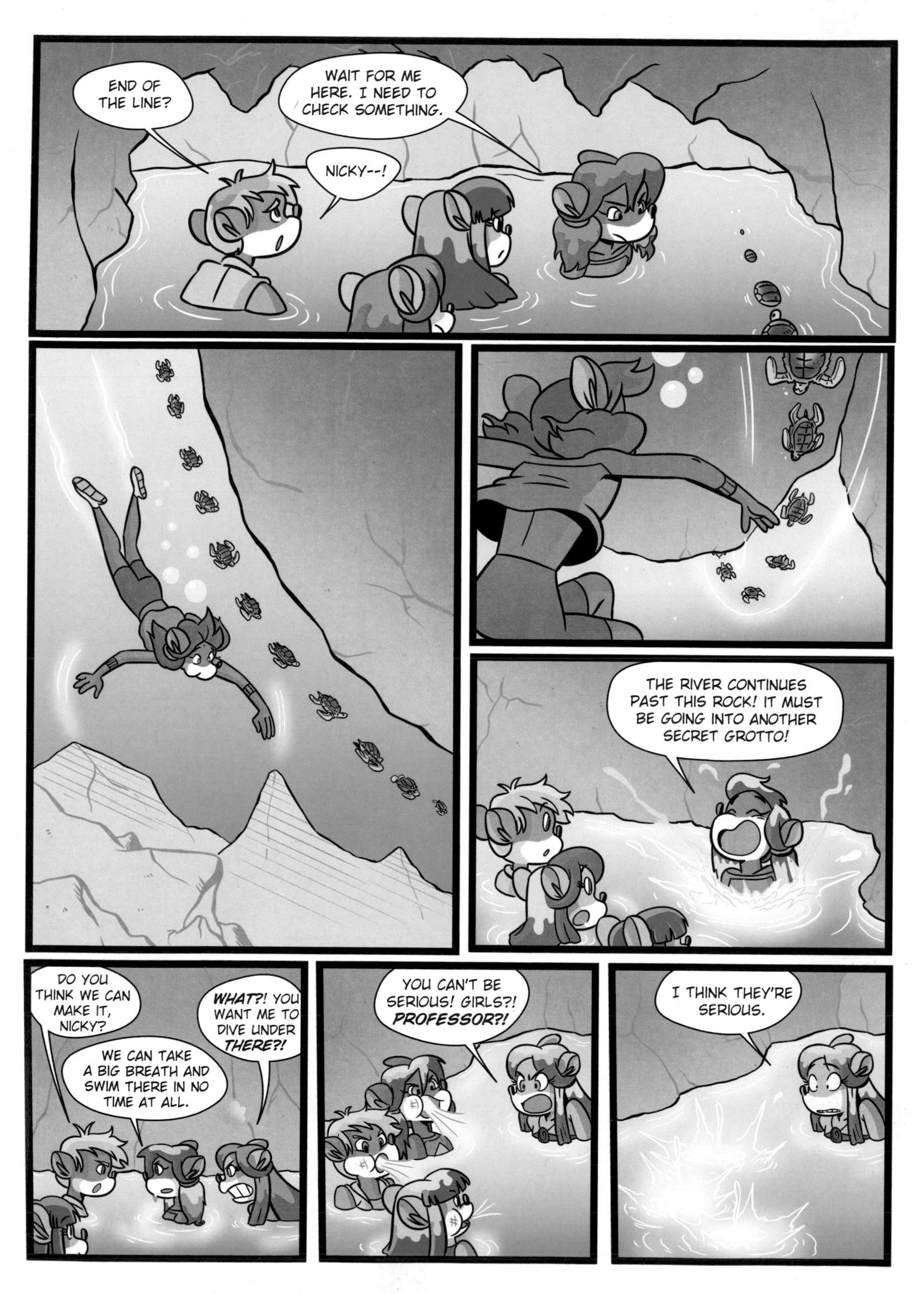

END OF THE LINE?
WAIT FOR ME HERE. I NEED TO CHECK SOMETHING.
NICKY--!
THE RIVER CONTINUES PAST THIS ROCK! IT MUST BE GOING INTO ANOTHER SECRET GROTTO!
DO YOU THINK WE CAN MAKE IT, NICKY?
WE CAN TAKE A BIG BREATH AND SWIM THERE IN NO TIME AT ALL.
WHAT?! YOU WANT ME TO DIVE UNDER **THERE?!**
YOU CAN'T BE SERIOUS! GIRLS?! **PROFESSOR?!**
I THINK THEY'RE SERIOUS.

IT . . . IT . . .
IT'S INCREDIBLE!
THE TURTLES!

I WONDER WHY THEY CAME TO *THIS* GROTTO.
IT'S FULL OF GARBAGE TOO.
HEY, I THINK I'VE FIGURED IT OUT.
IT LOOKS LIKE THEY'RE TRAPPED!
WOW, LOOK HOW BIG THESE GUYS ARE!
THEY'RE BEAUTIFUL!
SO MUCH TRASH. WE HAVE TO MAKE SURE YOUR MOTHER CLEANS UP THIS AREA, TOO, VANILLA.
OH, I DON'T THINK THAT'LL BE A PROBLEM.
MY MOTHER WOULD DO *ANYTHING* TO STOP THE CULPRIT BEHIND THIS DISASTER--
--RICHARD MALEFACTOR!!!
?

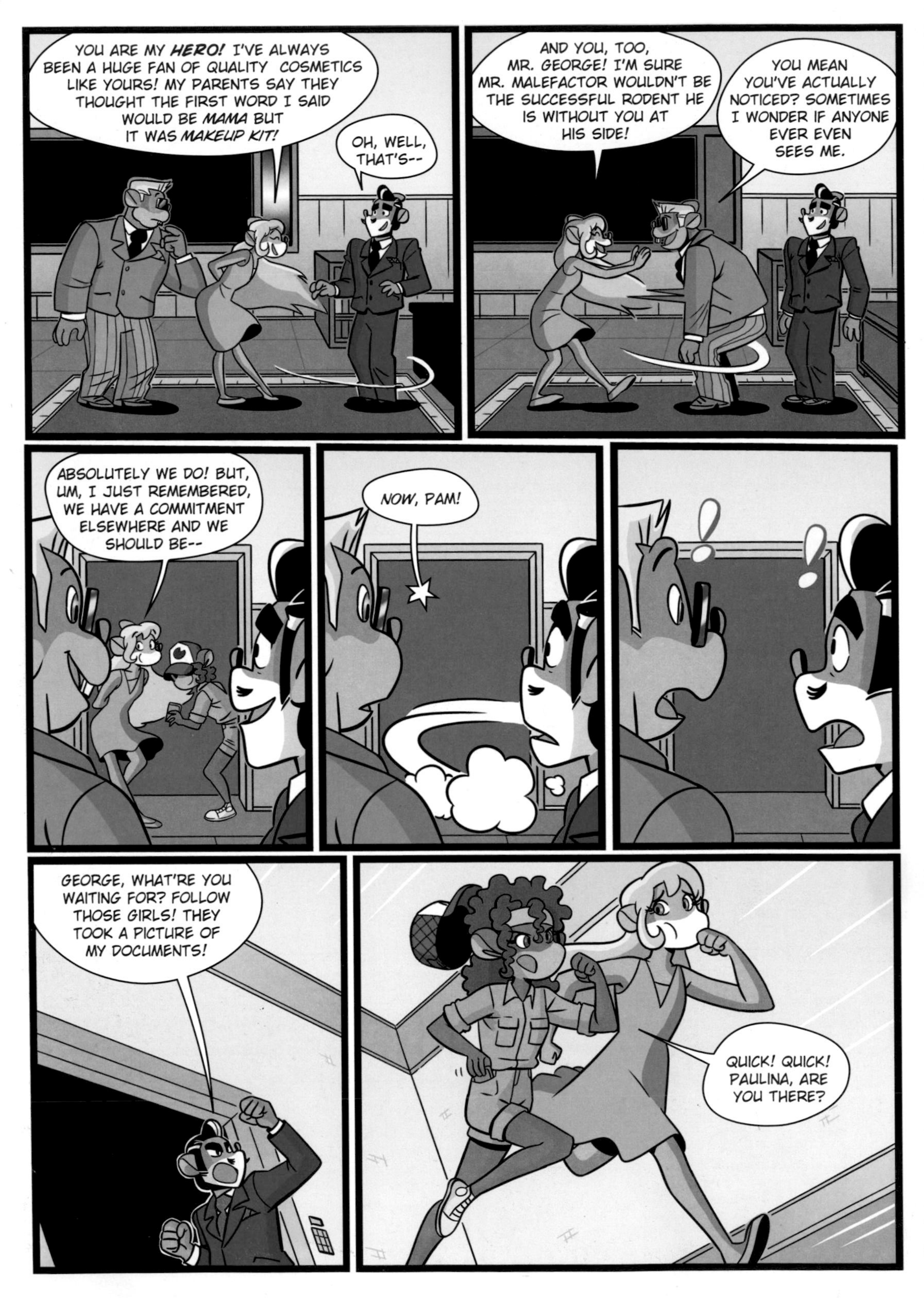
YOU ARE MY HERO! I'VE ALWAYS BEEN A HUGE FAN OF QUALITY COSMETICS LIKE YOURS! MY PARENTS SAY THEY THOUGHT THE FIRST WORD I SAID WOULD BE MAMA BUT IT WAS MAKEUP KIT!
OH, WELL, THAT'S--
AND YOU, TOO, MR. GEORGE! I'M SURE MR. MALEFACTOR WOULDN'T BE THE SUCCESSFUL RODENT HE IS WITHOUT YOU AT HIS SIDE!
YOU MEAN YOU'VE ACTUALLY NOTICED? SOMETIMES I WONDER IF ANYONE EVER EVEN SEES ME.
ABSOLUTELY WE DO! BUT, UM, I JUST REMEMBERED, WE HAVE A COMMITMENT ELSEWHERE AND WE SHOULD BE--
NOW, PAM!
!
!
GEORGE, WHAT'RE YOU WAITING FOR? FOLLOW THOSE GIRLS! THEY TOOK A PICTURE OF MY DOCUMENTS!
QUICK! QUICK! PAULINA, ARE YOU THERE?

COMPLIMENTS ON THE DIVERSION, COLETTE! NOW YOU NEED TO GET TO THE ROOF.
THE ROOF? ARE YOU SURE?
GRR . . . !
TRUST ME! AT THE END OF THE HALLWAY, THERE'S A METAL DOOR. OPEN IT.
METAL DOOR. I SEE IT!
HURRY, COLETTE!
OUCH!
WE'RE TRAPPED! WHAT DO WE DO, PAULINA?

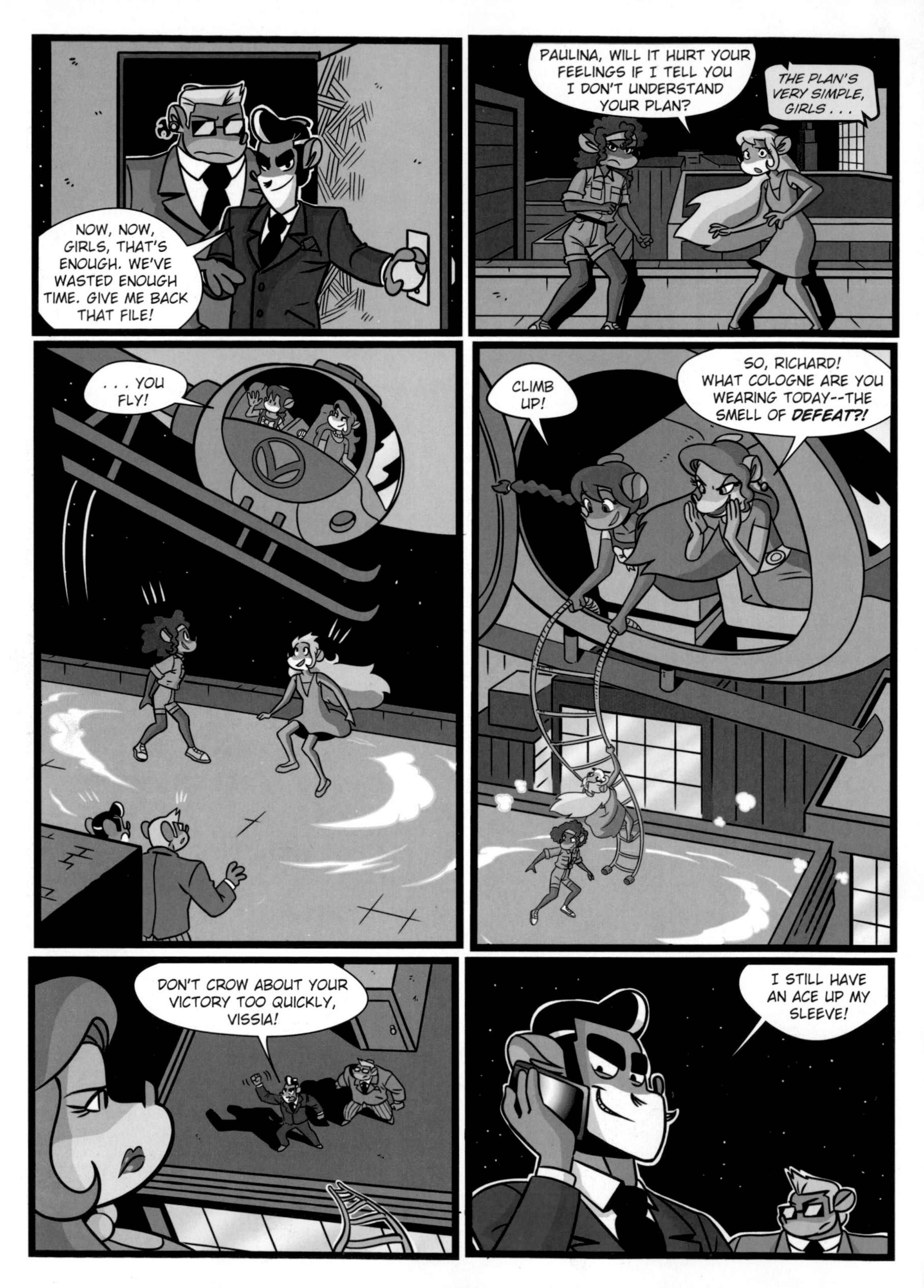
NOW, NOW, GIRLS, THAT'S ENOUGH. WE'VE WASTED ENOUGH TIME. GIVE ME BACK THAT FILE!
PAULINA, WILL IT HURT YOUR FEELINGS IF I TELL YOU I DON'T UNDERSTAND YOUR PLAN?
THE PLAN'S VERY SIMPLE, GIRLS . . .
. . . YOU FLY!
CLIMB UP!
SO, RICHARD! WHAT COLOGNE ARE YOU WEARING TODAY--THE SMELL OF DEFEAT?!
DON'T CROW ABOUT YOUR VICTORY TOO QUICKLY, VISSIA!
I STILL HAVE AN ACE UP MY SLEEVE!

JUST AFTER SUNSET, SOMEONE ON A SHIP GETS THE PHONE CALL . . .
DON'T WORRY, MR. MALEFACTOR. WE'LL TAKE CARE OF IT RIGHT AWAY!
SET COURSE FOR TURTLE ISLAND! WE HAVE TO MAKE SURE THE AREA IS CLEAR!
RIGHT AWAY, CAPTAIN!
BUT ONCE NEAR THE ISLAND . . .
THAT'S NOT RIGHT!
IT MUST'VE BEEN THE TIDES, CAPTAIN . . .
. . . THAT PULLED THE JETSAM OUT OF THE GROTTO!
HURRY! THOSE BUSYBODIES WILL BE HERE ANY MINUTE!
BUT WHAT'LL WE DO, CAPTAIN?
DROP ANCHOR AND START THE FORWARD ENGINES. IT WON'T TAKE LONG!

MEANWHILE, INSIDE THE GROTTO . . .
COME ON, GIRLS! JUST A LITTLE MORE EFFORT AND WE'LL BE THERE!
IF WE HAD TWO MORE PAWS TO HELP WE'D ALREADY BE FINISHED!
OH, VANILLA?
DON'T EVEN THINK ABOUT IT. I'M NOT HERE TO WORK!
NO KIDDING!
SHH, GIRLS-- DID YOU HEAR THAT?
VROOM
IT SOUNDS LIKE . . . A SHIP'S ENGINES! COULD IT BE OUR FRIENDS?
VROOM
UM . . . I'D SAY DEFINITELY *NOT!*
MORE TRASH?
I DON'T BELIEVE IT! DO THEY THINK THIS PLACE IS A ***DUMP?***

HEY, YOU OUT THERE! DO YOU HEAR ME?! WE'RE IN HERE! COME HERE AND GET US, RIGHT NOW!
IT'S USELESS, VANILLA. THEY CAN'T HEAR US OUT THERE. AND MAYBE THAT'S A GOOD THING . . .
KROOM
KROOM
KROOM
". . . JUST THINK OF HOW MUCH DAMAGE THEY COULD DO TO THIS GROTTO!"
ISN'T WHAT WE'RE DOING DANGEROUS?
ON THE CONTRARY!
WE'RE PROTECTING MR. MALEFACTOR.
AND PROTECTING HIM MEANS PROTECTING OURSELVES!
WE CAN'T DO THIS ALONE! THERE'S TOO MUCH GARBAGE!
VANILLA! ARE YOU GOING TO DO THE RIGHT THING AND GIVE US A HAND?
ALL RIGHT, ALL RIGHT! I CAN'T TAKE ANY MORE OF YOUR PESTERING! THERE, I'LL GET A COUPLE OF BITS HERE AND--
WHAT--?!

PLEASE DON'T HURT US, NICE TURTLES!!!
GIRLS, I DON'T KNOW HOW-- BUT WE DID IT!
"THE TURTLES CAN BREAK FREE NOW!"

TURN OFF THE ENGINES! MISSION ACCOMPLISHED! MR. MALEFACTOR WILL BE VERY PLEASED!
CAPTAIN, WE'VE GOT VISITORS!
GRR! IT'S THE BUSYBODIES THE BOSS WAS TALKING ABOUT!
EVEN IF THEY HAVE THAT FILE, THEY CAN'T ACCUSE US OF ANYTHING!

ISN'T IT A BIT LATE FOR A BOAT TOUR NEAR THE COAST OF TURTLE ISLAND?
I WAS THINKING THE SAME THING ABOUT SOMEONE GOING OUT IN A HELICOPTER AT THIS HOUR. YOU NEVER KNOW WHAT MIGHT HAPPEN!
I HEAR THIS IS THE BEST TIME TO GO FISHING FOR CROOKS WHO THROW GARBAGE INTO THE WATER!
REALLY? LET ME KNOW IF YOU FIND ANY PROOF MY SHIP HAD ANY GARBAGE!
SOMETHING IS MOVING DOWN THERE!
WOW-- LOOK AT WHAT'S COMING OUT OF THE CAVE!
ALL THOSE TURTLES HAVE BEEN IN THERE?
LOOK--THEY'RE LEAVING!

I DO BELIEVE IT'S TIME TO SEND FOR THE PRESS AGAIN TO SEE ALL THE GARBAGE FROM *YOUR* SHIP!
GIRLS, I'M GETTING WORRIED. WHERE ARE PROFESSOR VAN KRAKEN AND THE OTHERS?
EXCUSE ME, YOU UP THERE ON THE SHIP!
PERMISSION TO COME ABOARD?
IT'S THEM!
ARE YOU OKAY?
WE'RE GREAT!
THIS IS GREAT?
AH-AH-AH-CHOOo!!!
YOU CAN FEEL PROUD OF YOURSELF, VANILLA! THANKS TO YOU, TOO, THE TURTLES ARE SAFE!
IT'S TRUE. IT WAS A TEAM EFFORT!
WE'LL TELL YOU EVERYTHING! HOW'D IT GO HELPING VISSIA?
FANTASTIC! WE VISITED MR. MALEFACTOR'S BUILDING!
WELL . . . IT WASN'T REALLY A "VISIT" . . .

. . .BUT THE IMPORTANT THING IS THAT EVERYTHING TURNED OUT FOR THE BEST.
RIGHT, WHO WOULD'VE EVER GUESSED . . .
CHANNEL 6 NEWS
. . . THAT THE DE VISSEN FAMILY WOULD MAKE A CONTRIBUTION TO SAVING TURTLE ISLAND?
ES MALEFACTOR FOUND GUILTY
DE VISSEN DECLARES MALEFACTOR FOUND GUIL
I WAS VERY DISTRESSED TO DISCOVER THE INVOLVEMENT OF MY COLLEAGUE RICHARD MALEFACTOR IN THIS DREADFUL INCIDENT.
GRR!
SAVING THE TURTLE COMMUNITY WAS MY FIRST PRIORITY.
I CAN ONLY HOPE THAT SIMILAR INCIDENTS NEVER HAPPEN AGAIN, AND THAT THIS SPLENDID LANDSCAPE CONTINUES TO REMAIN UNCONTAMINATED . . .
" . . . AND FOREVER FREE AND SAFE."
END.

Watch Out For PAPERCUTZ™

Welcome to the socially-conscious, sixth THEA STILTON graphic novel from Papercutz, those friendly folks dedicated to publishing great graphic novels for all ages. I'm Salicrup, *Jim Salicrup*, Editor-in-Chief and Personal Shopper for Vissia De Vissen.

One of the most confusing things about this particular series of graphic novels, is that Thea Stilton rarely appears in it. Instead, we're treated to the adventures of the "Thea Sisters," yet none of these young women are actually related to Thea Stilton or each other! Now, if you've seen our previous volumes, you'll know that Nicky, Pamela, Violet, Colette, and Paulina all attend Mouseford Academy on Whale Island. It's here that they all take Professor Thea Stilton's journalism class. Because they admire Thea so much, they formed a group (or a sorority) that they call the Thea Sisters. *Now* it all makes sense, I hope.

Speaking of journalism, what exactly is that? Once upon a time, a journalist was specifically a reporter for a newspaper. As new forms of media came along, journalists could be reporters for radio, television, and now, the Internet. Generally, a journalist's job is to report the news. Unlike a television news anchor, who mainly reads the news, journalists are the ones who go to where the news is happening and write about what they see.

Recently, on May 19, 2016, one week after he retired, broadcast journalist Morley Safer passed away. Like millions of other viewers I admired Mr. Safer for his journalistic skills and his way of simply telling a story. He was very good at what he did. The 84 year-old Safer, was a journalist for 60 years, 46 of them on the highly-rated and respected CBS "newsmagazine" 60 Minutes. According to reports, he was inspired to become a "foreign correspondent" after reading the works of author Ernest Hemingway, who was a foreign correspondent. Hemingway was also novelist, short story writer, and lead quite an adventurous life that influenced many others in addition to Morley Safer.

Other than Clark Kent (mild-mannered reporter for a great metropolitan newspaper), I'm not sure if we are exposed to many fictional journalists these days. Back in 1941, the very first comics story written by legendary comics creator Stan Lee (Co-creator of *Spider-Man*, *the X-Men*, *the Avengers*, as well as creator of THE ZODIAC LEGACY, the graphic novels of which are published by Papercutz) was "*'Headline' Hunter, Foreign Correspondent*." That's how glamorous and exciting being a journalist was back then.

Now is a particularly difficult time for print journalists, as many newspapers are struggling to survive. (Don't worry, Thea Stilton, and her brother, Geronimo, are both secure in their positions – she's a special correspondent and he's the editor-in-chief– at the *Rodent's Gazette*.) With so much news reported on TV and the Internet for free, fewer people than ever before are buying newspapers. But now, journalists are finding exciting new ways to report on the news from all over the world, as technology has made it possible for information to travel faster and to reach more people than ever before.

Being a journalist is still an exciting and important career, and it's great fun to watch the Thea Sisters tackle environmental issues in their graphic novels. Who knows, maybe one day, we'll be watching journalists report on big stories, and find out it was the Thea Sisters who inspired them? (Do you have a nose for news?) In the meantime, enjoy the preview of GERONIMO STILTON #17 "The Mystery of the Pirate Ship" on the following pages, and be sure to keep an eye out for the next thrilling THEA STILTON graphic novel!

Thanks,

JIM

Stay in Touch!

Email: salicrup@papercutz.com
Web: www.papercutz.com
Twitter: @papercutzgn
Facebook: PAPERCUTZGRAPHICNOVELS
Snailmail: Papercutz, 160 Broadway, Suite 700, East Wing, New York, NY 10038

Special Preview of GERONIMO STILTON #17 "Mystery of the Pirate Ship"!

UNCLE, IT'S JUST A STORY. YOU CAN'T LET IT SCARE YOU!
IT MAY BE JUST A STORY BENJAMIN, BUT TRAP TOLD IT SO WELL!
YOU'RE TOO KIND, COUSIN!
BUT I'M SUCH A SCATTERBRAIN! I FORGOT TO INTRODUCE MYSELF. MY NAME IS STILTON, *Geronimo Stilton*, AND I EDIT THE RODENT'S GAZETTE, THE MOST FAMOUSE PAPER ON MOUSE ISLAND!
THE RULE WAS THAT WE WERE ALL SUPPOSED TO TELL A STORY. WE DIDN'T INTERRUPT YOU WHEN YOU RECITED YOUR LIST OF YOUR ANTIQUE CHEESE RIND COLLECTION.
DON'T REMIND ME, THEA, OR I'LL FALL ASLEEP AGAIN!
YOU DIDN'T TELL ME THEY HAD TO BE ADVENTURE STORIES! HOW WAS I SUPPOSED TO KNOW?
GO ON, THEN, GERONIMO. TRY AGAIN!
YEAH, UNCLE, TELL US ANOTHER!

OKAY, THEN...
ONCE UPON...
...A TIME...
CRACK
A BEAR!
USE A LITTLE IMAGINATION, COUSIN. I COULD'VE JUST GONE ON WITH MY STORY!
NO, NO! A BEAR!

ROOOAAAWR!
AHHH!
SAVE YOURSELVES! I'LL SLOW IT DOWN!
EN GARDE!
ROAR!
MY CHEESE!
QUICK, CLIMB UP A TREE TO SAFETY!
EASY FOR YOU TO SAY...

Don't Miss GERONIMO STILTON #17 "Mystery of the Pirate Ship"!

MB Mar 2017
YES, YES, OF COURSE, NATURALLY--THE TURTLES! I WAS THINKING ABOUT THE POOR TURTLES!
Vissia de Vissen
is no stranger to the Thea Sisters. Usually, she's causing the problems, but this time, she wants to help. Or does she?
WHO COULD HAVE SPOILED THIS MARVELOUS BEACH? A UNIQUE VISTA RUINED BY THE WORST KIND OF SCOUNDREL!
VANILLA, COME LOOK! THERE'S CLEARLY SOMEONE RESPONSIBLE FOR THIS TRASH!
I KNOW SOMEONE WHO'LL WANT TO COME HERE IN PERSON AND TELL EVERYONE ABOUT IT!
Vic and Vanilla de Vissen
are the spoiled children of Vissia. They're only too happy to help their mother do anything she asks – even if it's not a good deed!